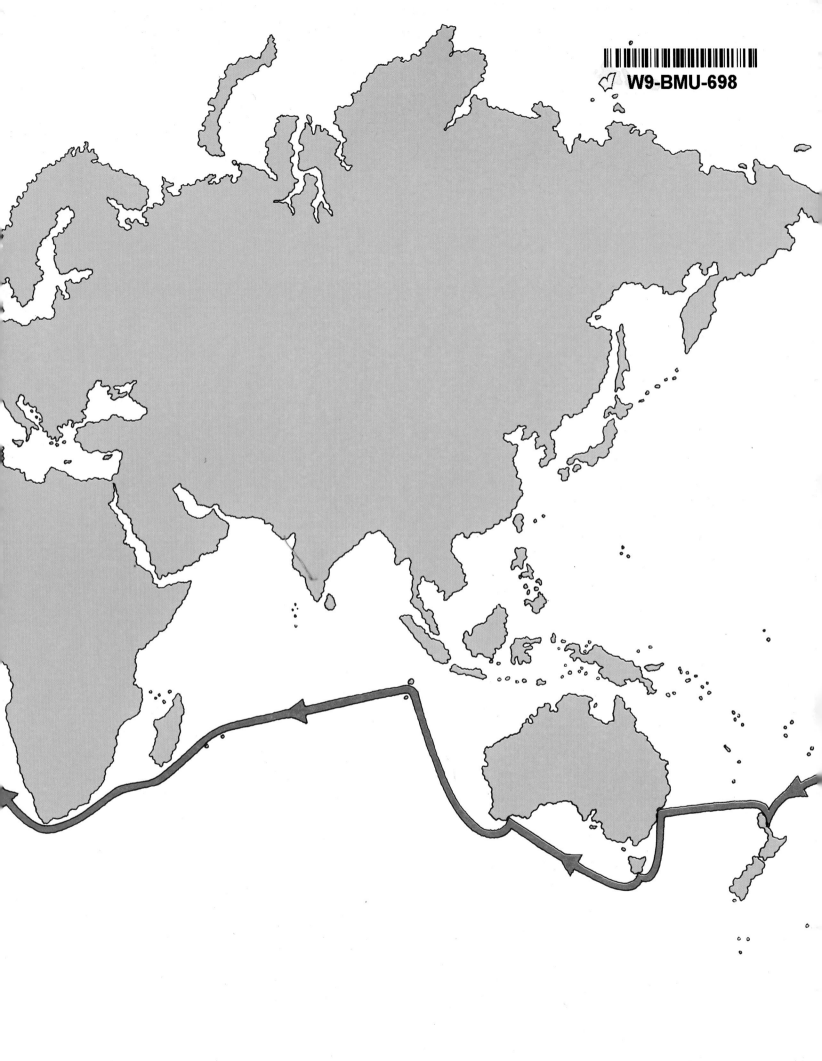

DARWIN

Nature Reinterpreted

Piero Ventura

DARWIN
Nature Reinterpreted

Text by Gian Paolo Ceserani

with the collaboration of Marisa Murgo
Translated by Kathleen Leverich

Houghton Mifflin Company
Boston 1995

Copyright © 1993 by Arnoldo Mondadori Editore S.p.A.
First American edition 1995
Originally published in Italy in 1993 by Mondadori
English translation by Kathleen Leverich copyright © 1995 by
Houghton Mifflin Company

Library of Congress Cataloging-in-Publication Data
Ventura, Piero.
  [Darwin e la riscoperta della natura. English]
  Darwin, nature reinterpreted / Piero Ventura ; text by
Gian Paolo Ceserani ; with the collaboration of Marisa Murgo ;
translated by Kathleen Leverich. — 1st American ed.
      p.   cm.
  Includes index.
  ISBN 0-395-70738-2 : $16.95
  1. Darwin, Charles, 1809-1882—Juvenile literature.
2. Naturalists—England—Biography—Juvenile literature.
3. Evolution (Biology)—Juvenile literature. [1. Darwin, Charles,
1809-1882. 2. Naturalists. 3. Evolution.] I. Ceserani, Gian
Paolo. II. Murgo, Marisa. III. Title.
QH31.D2V3613   1995
575'.0092—dc20   94-29989
[B]   CIP
                                            AC

Printed in Spain by Artes Gráficas Toledo, S.A.
    10 9 8 7 6 5 4 3 2 1
D.L.TO: 1137-1994

CONTENTS

MOTHER NATURE

Humans have always held two opposing views of the natural world. On one hand the Earth has been Mother Earth, the sacred wellspring of life. On the other it has been the quarry from which we extract whatever raw materials serve our industrial and technological needs. Only recently have we come to realize that Earth's resources are finite and that their depletion will destroy the natural world that gave us life and sustains us.

The destruction of natural environments is not a recent development. Ancient shipbuilders felled so many of Lebanon's famed cedars that today only a few dozen of those trees remain. The ancient Romans, too, destroyed entire forests to build their fleets. Intensive agriculture has also led to environmental disasters. Centuries of overcultivation by Middle Eastern farmers led to the formation of the region's vast deserts.

The idea of the Earth as mother, however, served as a powerful check on these human excesses, at least until the seventeenth century, when this compelling maternal image began to lose its potency.

The mining industry provides a good example. While the ancient Romans developed important mining operations, writers such as Seneca and Pliny deplored it as a violation of Mother Earth. Ancient African peoples also mined, but after having extracted minerals they refilled their miles-long caverns with stones. They wanted to "heal" the "wounds" they had made in Mother Earth. In the seventeenth century, mining became widespread in Europe. Far from being viewed as a wounding of the Earth, it was welcomed as "progress."

Following the seventeenth century's industrial revolution, Europeans began to alter the Earth's environment ever more drastically. But the same forces that brought about these changes—the Enlightenment, colonial expansion, scientific discoveries—also gave Europeans a new regard for nature and a desire to understand it more completely.

From 1600 on, mining operations grew steadily more complex. Miners worked in shafts hundreds of feet beneath the Earth's surface.

LINNAEUS

Carolus Linnaeus exemplified the new regard for the natural world. Linnaeus was born in southern Sweden in 1707 and lived during a period in which educated Europeans were looking at the world around them with new interest. These people wanted to pursue natural history in a precise and progressive manner. What they lacked was a scientific method of observation and classification. A standard system of plant nomenclature did not exist. Linnaeus's family was of modest means, but he succeeded in earning a degree in medicine. While still a student, he developed a classification system to order the immense world of plant and animal varieties.

Linnaeus's system classified plants according to the characteristics of their reproductive organs. He gave every plant two Latin names. The first name, or genus, indicated a group of similar plants. The second name, or species, was usually an adjective that described a specific subgroup. For example, the *Anemone*

A page of the Systema Naturae. *According to Linnaeus's system, the plant kingdom was divided into two categories: plants with visible reproductive organs and plants with nonvisible ones.*

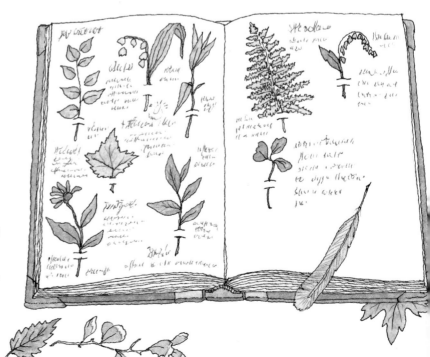

japonica is a plant of the genus *Anemone* and the species *japonica*. That is, it is an anemone native to Japan.

The system is an artificial one. Linnaeus himself noted that its classifications are based on a few exterior characteristics. He stressed that an organic system would be more useful. But he wisely concluded that "in the meantime, until an organic system is discovered, the artificial systems remain indispensable." His treatise, *Systema Naturae*, appeared in 1735 and enjoyed immediate success.

Parks and gardens were being created in England, and new plants were arriving in Europe regularly from Asia, Africa, and the Americas. A system was needed to name them, and Linnaeus had supplied it. He would later extend his system to the animal kingdom.

Linnaeus became a celebrated figure among his European contemporaries, many of whom were amateur naturalists who had created herbariums from plants gathered on expeditions in the woods and countryside. He received letters and packages containing seeds from all over the world. On visits to France and England he was welcomed as royalty. His fame spread even to the American colonies.

At home in Sweden Linnaeus taught at the University of Uppsala and received many honors. He died in 1778. Today we consider him one of the greatest naturalists of all time. His system is still the most commonly used method of classification. Linnaeus perceived a unity beyond the diversity of the natural world. He succeeded in his ambition "to gaze into the laboratory of God."

At home in Sweden, Linnaeus taught at the University of Uppsala.

CROSSING AMERICA

Explorers were fascinated by the vastness of the North American continent. From the 1500s on, they arrived to chart its majestic landscapes, waterways, and mountain chains. French explorers included Jacques Cartier, who navigated the Saint Lawrence River in 1534, Samuel de Champlain, who founded Quebec in 1608, Étienne Brulé and Robert La Salle, who traveled in the Great Lakes and explored Louisiana and Mississippi. In 1609 British explorer Henry Hudson discovered the river that bears his name. His compatriot Alexander Mackenzie became the first European to cross the continent, north of Mexico, by land.

Even more adventurous was the three-year expedition undertaken by U.S. Army Captains Meriwether Lewis and William Clark. President Thomas Jefferson had pressed for their expedition. Its purpose was to discover the source of the Missouri River and to establish a trail through

Lewis and Clark crossed unspoiled lands whose only inhabitants were Native Americans.

the Rocky Mountains to the Pacific coast.

Lewis and Clark left Saint Louis in a warship on May 14, 1804. Their expedition began in high spirits. Lewis's diary describes a natural paradise where bison herds numbered in the hundreds of thousands of animals. Elk were so unafraid of humans that they had to be driven off with sticks. Grizzly bears roamed the forests.

The company arrived at last at the Rocky Mountains, "the object of our hopes." With a Shoshone Indian as their guide, the explorers entered the great mountain chain on foot. There, troubles began.

Food grew scarce. The cold was unbearable. Expedition members were forced to eat their horses to survive. They endured terrible hardships, to arrive at last at the mountain barrier's final peak. A beautiful plain spread before them. They descended and five weeks later reached the Pacific.

In all, the Lewis and Clark expedition covered more than eight thousand miles.

A PRESIDENT'S GARDEN

Thomas Jefferson authored the Declaration of Independence. He served as U.S. president for two terms (1801-1809), during which he inaugurated the nation's new capital, Washington, D.C., and sponsored the Lewis and Clark expedition of 1804-1807. Jefferson was a highly educated man and a gifted architect. He collaborated on the plan for the U.S. Capitol building and he designed his own home, Monticello, in Charlottesville, Virginia.

16

Monticello, the Virginia estate designed by Thomas Jefferson.

At Monticello Jefferson indulged a lifelong passion: gardening. Another former president, George Washington, also was an accomplished gardener and landscape designer. At his Virginia home, Mount Vernon, Washington thinned the trees that lined the Potomac River to create a beautiful prospect. He built verandas to take advantage of the finest views. Both Washington and Jefferson were influenced by the designs of classical Italian gardens. Monticello is, after all, an Italian name. But each man put a distinctive imprint on his project.

Jefferson was determined that his gardens should be useful as well as beautiful. He laid out extensive vegetable gardens and orchards and continually adapted the spacious estate's plans to take advantage of new information and horticultural advances. Today Monticello is maintained as it was in Jefferson's time. Impressive as it is, it reflects only a small part of its farsighted owner's many plans. As a dedicated amateur botanist, Jefferson collected quantities of rare plants and seeds, primarily English varieties, which he cultivated in several nurseries. But he valued native species above all his exotic specimens and saw to it that Virginia's trees and shrubs formed the largest part of Monticello's plantings.

Jefferson cultivated hollies, rhododendrons, and magnolias as well as citrons, oranges, and figs. He showed that a dedicated amateur could surround himself with nature at its loveliest.

HUMBOLDT THE TEACHER

Baron Alexander von Humboldt, born in Berlin in 1769, was only thirty years old when he completed a major voyage of scientific exploration in tropical North and South America. Humboldt made a lengthy stay in the Orinoco River basin. He ventured as far as Bogotá, Colombia, and Quito, Ecuador. He navigated the Guayas River by barge, crossed the Andes Mountains, and climbed Ecuador's 20,561-foot Mount Chimborazo. He then traveled north to study Mexico's Pacific coast. Thirty years later, in 1829, he undertook an expedition through Eurasia's Ural and Altay mountains and around the Caspian Sea on behalf of Russia's Czar Nicholas I.

Humboldt was the last of the great amateur travelers and the first of the explorer scientists. His accounts of his travels are of importance not only for their scientific data, but also for what they reveal about the outlook of Western

Alexander von Humboldt and his company cross the Guayas River on a barge.

Europeans in the early 1800s. Europeans sought a closer acquaintance with nature and a more complete understanding of its processes.

Humboldt's books made an enormous impression on the next generation of aspiring naturalists. His *Voyage to the Equatorial Regions of the New Continent*, in twenty-three volumes, was the chief source of inspiration for the young Charles Darwin. Darwin would join an expedition to South America largely on the strength of it, and throughout the voyage he would check Humboldt's recorded impressions against his own firsthand observations. When Darwin sat down to write an account of his voyage, he took Humboldt's work as his model.

Humboldt made many farsighted observations. For instance, the role of humans in disrupting the natural world was clear to him. As an example he noted that the plants and animals European colonialists brought to the New World were frequently responsible for driving out local species.

Humboldt saw far beyond the common horizon of his day.

The facade of Christ's College, Cambridge University, from which Charles Darwin graduated in 1831.

CHARLES DARWIN

Few individuals have altered the intellectual landscape of their day as profoundly as Charles Darwin. Darwin's theory of evolution caused a scandal in the 1860s and remains a provocative topic today. Darwin was the first Western scientist to see nature as an interdependent whole and humans as one life form among many. This intellectual revolutionary was, in his daily life, a calm, methodical person.

Darwin was born on February 12, 1809, into an affluent English family. His paternal grandfather Erasmus Darwin was a noted physician, poet, and theoretician. The Darwin family were close relations of the Wedgwoods, proprietors of the famous china firm.

Darwin's father, Robert, a well-known doctor, wanted his son to follow him into medical practice. In 1826 Charles began his medical studies at Edinburgh University in Scotland, but he quickly developed a passion for natural history. When a freed black slave from Guiana, South America, taught him avian taxidermy and told him stories of the tropical rain forests, Darwin's interest was intense. He passed time on the Scottish coast, scouring the ocean bottom for small marine animals to study.

Although Darwin hated his medical studies, the university's intellectual environment suited him. One of his teachers, Edmond Robert Grant, taught that all creatures, from humans to polyps, have some organs in common. At the time such theories were considered blasphemy. Darwin left Edinburgh and medical school in 1827 without a degree. He continued his studies at Christ's College, Cambridge University, where he found the atmosphere more conservative and to his mind less stimulating. Nevertheless he remained and graduated in 1831. Even at Cambridge he continued his natural history outings.

THE GREAT OPPORTUNITY

In his early twenties Charles Darwin found himself wondering what his life's profession should be. He had no doubts about his true vocation: he wanted to be a scholar of the natural sciences. But he had to earn a living.

The best plan seemed to be to become a country parson of the Anglican church. Darwin had little interest in the church, but a parson's life would offer all the peace and security necessary to a scholar. Darwin was prepared to follow that course eventually. For the present he was content to relax at home in the company of his brothers and sisters and of the even larger Wedgwood clan.

The quiet country life, however, could not satisfy the intellectually restless Darwin. He passed his time in natural history rambles, in serious geology studies, and in considering a voyage to the Canary Islands. Humboldt's

books had aroused his interest, and the Canaries seemed the most accessible of the fabled explorer's destinations.

At just this moment, Darwin received a proposal. The British Admiralty was looking for someone to accompany Captain Robert FitzRoy on a voyage of exploration along the South American coast. FitzRoy, who was twenty-six, wanted a "young gentleman" who might keep him company and join him at the table. Naval discipline isolated the captain from his crew, and it would have been unwise for FitzRoy to attempt the two-year voyage with no companion aboard. Darwin seemed perfectly suited to the position. He was of the right social class, and although not a professional naturalist, he knew geology, biology, and botany. He could skin and stuff animals, and he was a fine shot. For Darwin, it was the

22

opportunity of a lifetime. He would have jumped at it except for one worry: What would his father, the strict Dr. Robert Darwin, say?

Naturally the doctor said no. The desperate Charles sought the Wedgwoods' help. They took his side, and Dr. Darwin reluctantly gave in. Charles could not contain his joy. He traveled to London to meet FitzRoy. The captain had a reputation for brusqueness. He was, however, courteous and loyal. The two men immediately liked one another.

FitzRoy explained the aims of the voyage to Darwin. The English had many commercial interests in South America, and these required a more precise knowledge of the coastline. The expedition's task was to produce accurate charts. A naturalist would make a welcome addition to the company.

There were various problems, and FitzRoy listed them bluntly. Darwin would have to pay for his own expenses. The voyage had been extended from two years to three. (It would end up lasting for five years, however.) Meals would be frugal; Darwin's quarters, narrow and uncomfortable.

It would have taken a good deal more to discourage Darwin. He rushed to put together his kit. His first acquisitions were a telescope, compass, rifle, and pistol.

Science and adventure: these would be the voyage's dual themes.

Darwin's family were members of England's landed gentry, as were his relatives the Wedgwoods.

THE *BEAGLE*

FitzRoy took Darwin to see the *Beagle*. The captain quickly understood that his future companion had not realized how small a brigantine was. The ship was only ninety feet long and twenty-four feet wide. In spite of its modest dimensions, it had a displacement of 350 tons, and its three decks housed a crew of sev-

enty-three. The design of its sails, distribution of cargo, inclination of masts, and tension of its rigging made it an exceptionally responsive vessel. "A wise creature," Darwin would later pronounce the ship.

FitzRoy wasn't sparing any expense on its refitting. The old boat was being furnished with a new deck, a modern galley, advanced lightning rods, and brass cannons rather than iron

The Beagle *was ninety feet long and twenty-four feet wide. Seventy-three human beings inhabited its cramped spaces during the ship's voyage around the world.*

ones, which might interfere with the compasses.

Darwin was struck by a contrast. Mahogany fittings gleamed everywhere, and the ship's furnishings were luxurious, but space was severely cramped. The cabin assigned to him had such a low ceiling that the six-foot Darwin had to stoop inside it. During the day Darwin would share the cabin's very limited desk space with the ship's two cartographers. At night the tiny cabin would be all his. It was the only single cabin besides the captain's. The one drawback was that Darwin would have to sleep in a hammock.

Darwin liked the officers to whom he was introduced. The crew was young—the oldest member was just over thirty. Darwin forced himself to think of the *Beagle* not as a claustrophobic conveyance but as a lively community.

A DIFFICULT DEPARTURE

Darwin found the next few months onshore more difficult than all the hardships that he would endure during the five-year voyage that followed. Five times Captain FitzRoy was forced to postpone the departure. Once, the *Beagle* had to return to port because of impassable seas. Darwin became increasingly anxious. He took advantage of the delays to go to London for scientific instruments he lacked and to familiarize himself with both the ship and his tiny cabin. His family shared his worries, and Darwin had time to realize how much he would miss their affection and his comfortable home.

His anxieties were cut short two days after Christmas, 1831. The seventy-three-man *Beagle* crew awakened to splendid weather.

FitzRoy gave the order, and the crew sprang into action. They were finally under way. Darwin's exultation quickly turned to despair when he took to his hammock with seasickness. It was a terrible prospect for someone who would be living on a ship for several years. His only solace was to read Humboldt's descriptions of the tropics. On January 16, 1832, the *Beagle* made port at Saint Jago in the Cape Verde Islands. It was a desolate, volcanic landscape, but for Darwin it was paradise. Here Humboldt's words became real. The young naturalist was fascinated by the tangle of tropical vegetation. Palms. Baobabs. Liana vines, around which kingfishers fluttered while jungle cats slipped among the enormous tree trunks.

Ecstatic that his dreams were being realized,

26

The Beagle *anchored off Saint Jago in the Cape Verde Islands on January 16, 1832. It was Darwin's first contact with an "exotic" land.*

Darwin searched the shore, collecting brilliantly colored sponges and splendid corals. But what was that up there? Thirty feet above sea level a white stripe appeared in the cliffs. It was a sedimentary layer of compressed shells and coral. Darwin asked himself the first of many questions that would trouble him throughout the voyage: What were shells and coral doing at such a height? The ocean had not receded. Some cataclysm, therefore, must have raised the earth. It was the first of many theories he considered throughout the voyage.

27

THE BRAZILIAN RAIN FOREST

The *Beagle* set sail for Brazil and crossed the Equator on February 16, 1832. First-time crossers of "the line" were traditionally initiated in a raucous ceremony. Darwin was among those of the *Beagle* crew who were "baptised." The ship arrived at Bahia, Brazil, on February

Darwin crossed the Equator for the first time on February 16, 1832. Twelve days later the Beagle *reached Bahia, Brazil. From there the crew ventured into the rain forest.*

28

28, and Darwin experienced a joy even more intense than the one he had felt in Cape Verde. "The jungle," he wrote with emotion, "is a mixture of sounds and silences, like a great cathedral during Evensong." Enormous baobab trees welcomed him into their canopied passageways. Whistles, trills, croaks, and buzzes filled the air on every side.

The ship continued and one month later arrived in the bay of Rio de Janeiro. Here Darwin received his first letters from home. It was startling. The letters spoke of the familiar English countryside, tranquil country houses, and a life utterly different from the South American life and landscape before him. They spoke of the weddings of his many cousins. Darwin must have felt terribly remote from the existence that until a few months earlier had been his daily life.

In Brazil he had his first disagreement with FitzRoy. The subject was slavery, an institution widely practiced by the European colonials. Darwin was shocked by the manner in which slaves who had been transported in mass from Africa were treated. FitzRoy, an aristocrat whose views were decidedly more conservative, didn't find the matter so serious. The discussion erupted into a loud argument, and the short-tempered captain ordered Darwin from his cabin. But FitzRoy was a principled man. He realized that he had overreacted, and he apologized.

Darwin's relations with Augustus Earle, the expedition's painter, by contrast, were completely cordial. Earle accompanied Darwin on many shore trips and left us his detailed portraits of native animals and plants.

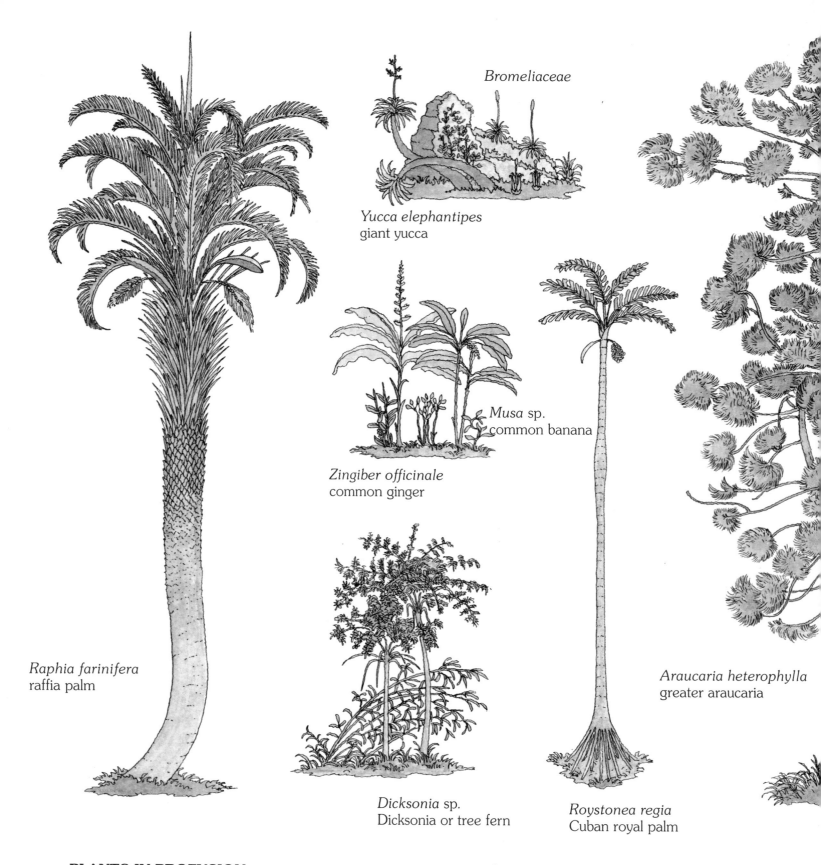

Bromeliaceae

Yucca elephantipes
giant yucca

Musa sp.
common banana

Zingiber officinale
common ginger

Raphia farinifera
raffia palm

Araucaria heterophylla
greater araucaria

Dicksonia sp.
Dicksonia or tree fern

Roystonea regia
Cuban royal palm

PLANTS IN PROFUSION

Darwin was fascinated by each of the tropical rain forests he visited, but the Brazilian forest stirred him most deeply. He wrote excitedly of the tangle of vegetation. "Twiners entwining twiners—tresses like hair—beautiful lepidopters—silence—Hosannah!"

In order to fully understand the sensations of a nineteenth-century European in the tropics, we must remember that Europe had been ravaged by the final Ice Age to a greater extent than any other part of the planet. More than 80 percent of local plant species had perished. Until the mid-seventeenth century, Europeans had never even glimpsed many of the plants that form our everyday landscape.

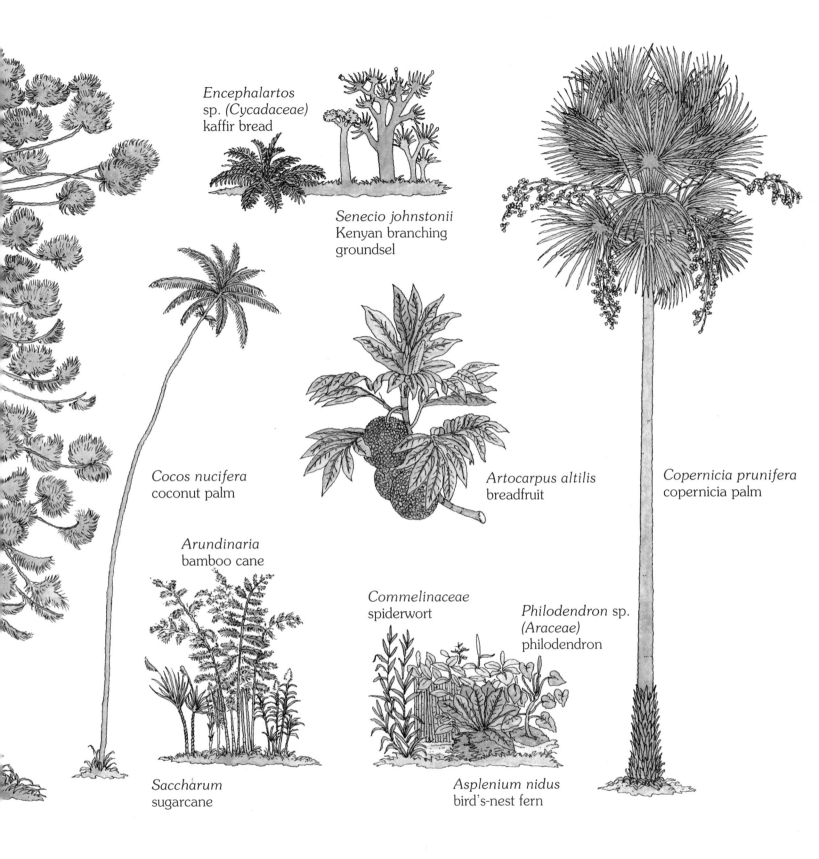

Encephalartos
sp. *(Cycadaceae)*
kaffir bread

Senecio johnstonii
Kenyan branching
groundsel

Cocos nucifera
coconut palm

Artocarpus altilis
breadfruit

Copernicia prunifera
copernicia palm

Arundinaria
bamboo cane

Commelinaceae
spiderwort

Philodendron sp.
(Araceae)
philodendron

Saccharum
sugarcane

Asplenium nidus
bird's-nest fern

Trade with Africa, Asia, and the Americas, combined with Europeans' growing interest in gardening, resulted in numerous expeditions by "plant hunters," who brought back to Europe the seeds of thousands of exotic species. Even a scientist like Darwin could not but be overcome by the tropics' beauty and diversity. But the naturalist in him took precedence over the mere appreciator.

As the voyage progressed, particularly through its stops in the Falklands and Galápagos islands, Darwin focused his attention on the patterns of plant diffusion and adaptation to local environments. This theme would become one of the keys to his theory of evolution.

31

GIANTS' BONES

The *Beagle* continued its voyage south. It reached Montevideo, Uruguay, on July 26, 1832. Darwin hoped to find some good fossils in South America, particularly since there was only one such relic in all of England. He believed that a significant find would more than justify his participation in the voyage. While on a visit to the pampas, Argentina's vast prairies with their cattle herds and gauchos, or cowboys, he had a stroke of good fortune. On a stretch of coast he discovered the fossilized bones of a gigantic mammal. The following day he found a huge cranium, and then a jaw whose single tooth showed it to be that of a megatherium, an enormous, extinct ground sloth.

Darwin lacked specific training in the zoology of ancient mammals. Knowledge of that subject in the 1830s was limited at best. Darwin asked himself these questions: Why had such immense animals become extinct?

What had happened eons ago to cause such a dramatic event?

Darwin had no answers. He had to be satisfied with carrying aboard the remains of at least six animals, including sloths, armadillos, and a guanaco—an animal related to the llama. He packed the fossils in crates for shipment to Cambridge. FitzRoy worried about this invasion of his ship's holds and remarked wryly on the "apparent rubbish" Darwin had brought aboard. In the following months and years he would become accustomed to such "rubbish." Darwin continued to seek and find fossils throughout the voyage. He wrote: "The pleasure of the first day of partridge shooting or the first day's hunting cannot be compared to finding a fine group of fossilized bones which tell their story of former times with almost a living tongue."

For Darwin the most important hunt had become the search for the truth of what had happened in the millions of years of life on Earth.

Darwin's discoveries of fossilized animals, millions of years old, continued throughout the voyage.

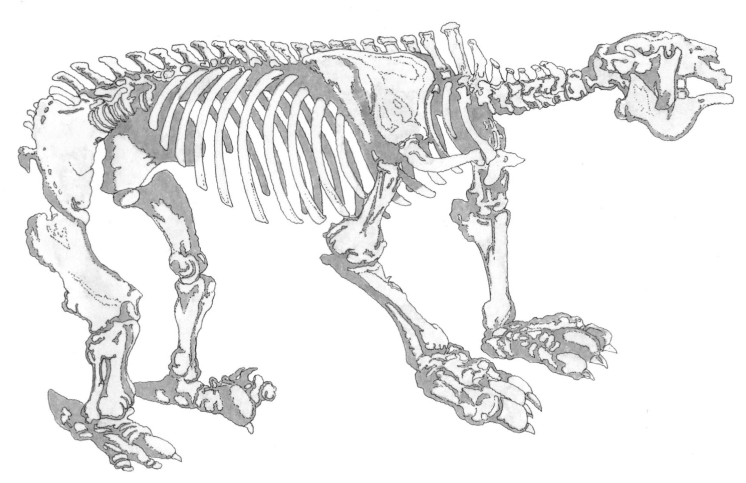

Reconstruction of a megatherium skeleton.

MASS EXTINCTIONS

Scientists can take a few bones or even bone fragments and reconstruct the gigantic animals that walked the Earth in past eras. The work of scientists like Darwin was fundamental, therefore, to our learning about Earth's history. Not all the questions that the young Darwin asked himself in 1832, however, had ready answers.

What, for example, caused the mass extinctions? Why did the dinosaurs who dominated terrestrial life millions of years ago perish?

Scientists have suggested a number of theories. The one that seems most likely is also the

34

Reconstruction of the skeleton of a mylodon.

most provocative: approximately every 20 million years a star disturbs the asteroid belt, and the Earth is battered by an asteroid storm. The violent event causes climatic changes that may destroy many species. The dinosaurs probably became extinct as a result of such a cataclysm.

Today's scientists have at their disposal convincing evidence. We know that the Earth underwent many catastrophic events, each of which has, as Darwin suspected, destroyed the majority of living species. Darwin lacked such evidence, but he guessed the truth.

Interior of Darwin's cabin on the Beagle.

TREASURE CHESTS

Darwin was startled when he saw his cabin on the *Beagle* for the first time. He called it "a tiny mahogany dressing room."

The details of Darwin's shipboard life were often amusing. At least that was the way Darwin, who had a good sense of humor, made them sound in his journal. Imagine a young man used to living in an enormous English country house confined to a small ship's cabin. One of his principal problems was learning how to get into his sleeping hammock. At first he tried to climb in from a table. The hammock swayed, and Darwin ended up on the floor. He finally realized that he needed to sit in the hammock first and swing his legs in afterward.

As time passed, Darwin managed to adapt to his floating home. He never, however, became a true seaman.

The ship's cramped quarters also proved to be a problem when Darwin began collecting, cataloging, and shipping his finds to Cambridge. Here is a summary of what this work in one location, Maldonado, Uruguay, included: capture of eighty species of birds; notation of habits, songs, and nesting places; stomach dissections to establish diet; cataloging and packing of fossils for shipment to England; capture of such large and small animals as rats, snakes, and deer; and shipment of their skeletons to England. The work was overwhelming. Darwin chose a young crew member, Syms Covington, as his assistant for the length of the voyage.

Back in England, Darwin's crates began to arrive regularly. The fossils excited great interest and were presented at a conference in Cambridge. Darwin's teacher, John Stevens Henslow, wrote to him, "The name of Darwin is destined for immortality." Darwin was beside himself with joy. He saw himself no longer as an amateur collector but as a true scientist, a theoretician capable of forming hypotheses from the ancient bones that seemed to tell him their stories. He came to believe that his observations, if accepted, would have great importance "for the theory of the earth's origin."

The work of cataloging and packing the fossils and other finds took much of the crew's time. Hundreds of crates were sent to England.

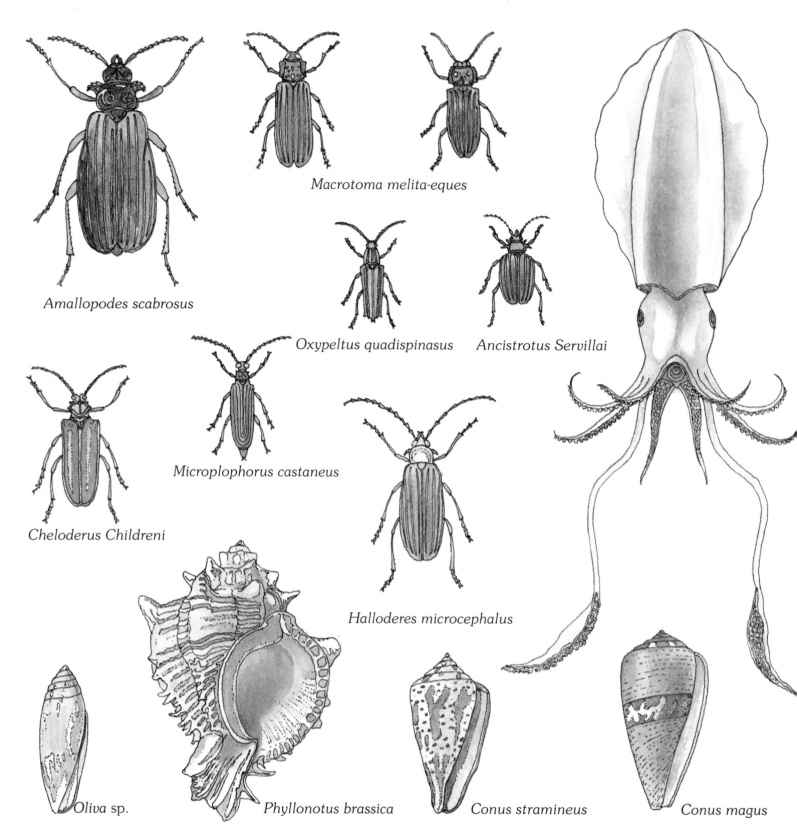

Amallopodes scabrosus

Macrotoma melita-eques

Oxypeltus quadispinasus

Ancistrotus Servillai

Cheloderus Childreni

Microplophorus castaneus

Halloderes microcephalus

Oliva sp.

Phyllonotus brassica

Conus stramineus

Conus magus

THE MINIATURE WORLD

Darwin's first public speaking engagement had been in 1827 at the Plinian Society, a naturalists' group in Edinburgh to which his teacher, Robert Edmond Grant, introduced him. There Darwin announced a discovery: The specks found inside empty oyster shells were leech eggs. This small discovery was the result of many hours spent scouring the Scottish coast for small marine creatures. Darwin correctly foresaw that the tiniest creatures harbored clues to the origins of life on Earth.

If the Scottish coast had been a fruitful hunting ground for the young scientist, the luxuriant ambiance of the tropics was a paradise. Once again he saw that Humboldt's descriptions were absolutely faithful. "Never have I felt so intense a joy. If I began by admir-

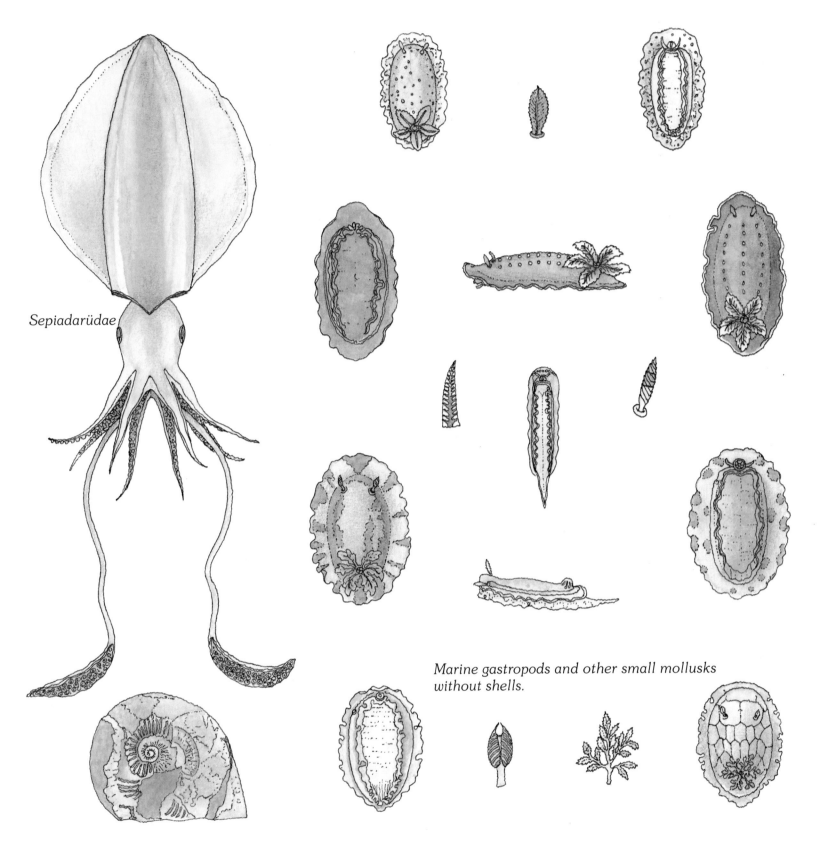

Sepiadarüdae

Marine gastropods and other small mollusks without shells.

ing Humboldt, now I nearly worship him. He alone knows how to describe what one feels upon arriving in the tropics. Currently I am enthralled by spiders. If I am not mistaken I have already captured examples of a new genus which I will be able to send to Cambridge."

But the countless species of beetles, spiders, and ants were not to interest Darwin as much as the members of "that ambiguous tribe" of marine organisms in which plants and animals seemed indistinguishable.

When he reached the Pacific's coral reefs, Darwin would spend entire days in the water collecting samples. As he examined the living coral under his microscope, he came to believe that at this basic level of life the plant and animal kingdoms must share a common origin.

39

PATAGONIA

While FitzRoy was absorbed in the painstaking work of charting the coast, Darwin temporarily left the *Beagle* to explore Argentina's pampas. He lived as the gauchos did, camping out each night under the stars, "with the sky as canopy." He had many encounters with indigenous wildlife, including giant anteaters, armadillos so swift at burrowing that he never managed to capture one, and a small rare species of ostrich that was later named for him, the Rhea darwini.

Back onboard ship, Darwin continued down the coast without any regrets about the country he was leaving behind. The Argentinian landscape *seemed* beautiful to him; the people in contrast, coarse.

The *Beagle* finally reached Patagonia, the southernmost region of the continent. This isolated land had entranced travelers who came before Darwin, and it would entrance those who came after him. It was desolate country, but its silence appealed to Darwin. Its solitude pleased him.

Patagonia's southern tip, Tierra del Fuego, was waterless desert. The only native mammal, the iguana, survived because it could drink saltwater. Enormous ice floes drifted north, past the coast, from Antarctica. Viewed from the hot, arid land, they made a breathtaking vision.

Darwin was struck by the local people. To his mind, they were semicivilized at best, with crude ways and red-painted faces. Yet they ate with spoons and forks. Darwin saw this use of simple technology as evidence of human beings' capacity to advance. He considered it proof that the chasm between a "savage" and a "civilized" person could be bridged. After all, the *Beagle* carried three Fuegians, natives of Tierra del Fuego, as passengers. They spoke English and dressed in the European manner. Darwin wondered how they would behave once disembarked in their own land.

Darwin and his companions were stunned by the contrast between luxuriant vegetation and ice floes in such proximity.

PRIMITIVE PEOPLES

The story of the three natives onboard the *Beagle* was unusual. On an earlier voyage FitzRoy had skirmished with the local people and taken some of them prisoner. Three were brought back to London, where they became the subjects of an experiment. This man, boy, and girl were given the names York Minster, Jemmy Button, and Fuegia Basket. When they disembarked in England, they were twenty-seven, fifteen, and ten years old, respectively. The English attempted to "civilize" them, teaching them English, Christianity, and how to use simple implements. A year later the experiment seemed to have succeeded. The Fuegians were even presented at the British court. FitzRoy was now charged with returning them to their homeland to see if civilization would take root and grow in that hostile world.

The captain guided the ship through a watery labyrinth. Darwin noted that the desolation of the place, where everything dripped with foul-smelling water, surpassed description. But what disconcerted him most was the sight of the Fuegians on shore. In contrast to York, Jemmy, and Fuegia, these were the most primitive people that a nineteenth-century

Three natives of Tierra del Fuego sailed aboard the Beagle. After a year's stay in England, they were taken back to their own country.

European could imagine. They seemed filthy and disheveled. Their voices sounded harsh. Darwin studied them with attention. "They do not know the meaning of having a house, much less of having domestic furnishings. They are ignorant of all that reason can achieve and good sense decide."

Where did these people come from? Why did they live in such a hostile environment? Darwin began to put his data in order. He reasoned that monkeys, primitive peoples, and philosophers were links in an uninterrupted progression of mental abilities. The enormous difference between the Fuegians and the Europeans convinced Darwin that progressive adaptations and improvements explained the gap between those at the bottom and those at the top of the evolutionary scale.

The three Europeanized Fuegians were dropped off in their native land, along with such "civilizing" gifts as chamber pots, tea trays, white linen, and crockery. The ship departed with plans to return some weeks later.

TRAUMATIC MOMENTS

Every voyage has moments a traveler dreads—storms, illnesses, disappointments. The *Beagle*'s voyage was no exception. The conclusion to the three Fuegians' story was one such event. When the ship returned to the Strait of Magellan to check on the fate of the three who had been put onshore, a Fuegian paddled a canoe alongside. It was Jemmy Button. Darwin noted, "I have never seen a transformation so complete and so horrifying."

Jemmy no longer wore clothes. His hair was long and matted. He looked like the Fuegians who had never been to England and seemed ashamed of his appearance. No sooner did he glimpse the captain than he turned away from the ship. When he was finally coaxed aboard, an uncontrollable wailing sounded from the canoe. It was Jemmy's new wife, who was afraid she had lost him forever. Before he left the ship for good, Jemmy told how Fuegia Basket and York Minster had fled taking with them all the "civilizing" gifts. He made his farewells without regrets and added that he had no intention of ever returning to England.

The incident left all aboard dismayed, and in this frame of mind they headed the ship west.

The *Beagle* now had a companion vessel. FitzRoy had acquired a smaller, rundown ship, the *Adventure*, which he had refitted. The *Adventure* helped with the surveying work. Together the two ships passed through the Strait of Magellan to explore South America's Pacific coast. Darwin was beside himself. His great desire was to reach the Andes.

Events, however, did not go smoothly. A terrible storm hit the *Beagle* and the *Adventure*. Darwin was more seasick than he had ever been, but during the hours when the storm raged, he learned to appreciate FitzRoy's considerable nautical skills. The rough and rude crew also respected the captain and admired his abilities.

Among all the events Darwin witnessed the one that impressed him the most was the earthquake that struck while the *Beagle* lay off the Chilean coast. The ship took refuge in the roiling seas, and when it later reached the city of Concepción it was greeted by an apocalyptic vision. Buildings lay in ruins everywhere. A ship had been lifted from the harbor and hurled into the streets. The cathedral, with its three-foot walls, was nearly leveled. The dead numbered in the hundreds.

Darwin wrote, "The world, the very emblem of all that is solid," moved underfoot ". . . like a crust over a fluid." In the space of two minutes it produced a profound sense of insecurity.

What struck Darwin most was evidence that

The Beagle, *along with its auxiliary ship* Adventure, *weathered a serious storm in the Strait of Magellan.*

The ruins of Concepción, Chile, as they appeared to Darwin following the violent earthquake of 1832.

the land had risen by more than three feet! That phenomenon might explain the sight he had observed in Argentina: shells compressed high in a cliff. The earth, he guessed, had risen through a series of convulsions over the course of millions and millions of years. That was why maritime fossils turned up in so many odd places. Time was the factor that explained all. Darwin felt small and almost insignificant in the face of the majestic pace at which the natural world evolved.

Exploring the Andes was the realization of
Darwin's long-cherished dream.

THE ANDES

Darwin had arrived on the Pacific coast and at last could realize his dream. He ventured into the Andes, the mountain range that runs the length of South America, the longest chain in the world.

Darwin's expedition proved worth the wait. The clear mountain air allowed him to view Chile spread like a vast topographic map at his feet. He judged the sight sublime and wrote, "I felt glad I was by myself." He roamed the mountains, marveling at each fantastic creature he encountered: pumas that attacked the legs of the llamalike guanacos; mice with coiled tails; a cloud of smoke that turned out to be a swarm of grasshoppers. He was not frightened even when caught in a mountain storm.

Darwin was particularly struck by the grand condors that took advantage of high-altitude air currents to soar without moving their wings.

Captured condors fetched a high price. Darwin witnessed how one was taken. The bird was lured with bait into an enclosure. Since a condor must run in order to take off, once inside the enclosure, it was trapped.

THE GALÁPAGOS ISLANDS

Galápago is the Spanish word for a giant species of tortoise. The name was also given to a group of islands situated five hundred miles off the South American coast. The islands were known primarily as a spot where ships put in to replenish their water supplies.

The *Beagle* crew found barren landscapes, unappealing beaches of volcanic black sand, and an oppressive atmosphere. The only habitation was a penal colony. Yet it was in these desolate islands that Darwin made the observations that would lead to his revolutionary theory.

The Galápagos swarmed with animal life.

48

Darwin's observations in the Galápagos were crucial to his development of a theory of evolution.

The water was full of sharks, tropical fish, and the famous tortoises. There were iguanas, cormorants, penguins, seals, and the finches that would form the basis of Darwin's reflections. What struck him most, however, were the tortoises. They stood as high as a man's chest and weighed as much as five hundred pounds. The one Darwin measured was over four feet long—large enough to ride, which Darwin did.

Darwin remained in the Galápagos for five weeks, one week with only Syms Covington as his companion. In that brief period he took the notes that years later would force a new interpretation of the origins of life on Earth.

Geospiza scandens
cactus ground finch

Zenaida galapagoensis
Galápagos dove

Ramphastos toco
toucan

Thraupis bonariensis darwini
Darwin's tanager

Magnirostris fortis
larger ground finch

Buteo galapagoensis
Galápagos hawk

Othos dentex
harlequinfish

Hypoplectodres nigrorubrum
black-banded sea perch

EYE-OPENING CREATURES

As a naturalist Charles Darwin was interested in every animal he encountered. The creatures that populated the Galápagos, however, would alter the course of his life and thoughts.

When later he began to arrange the specimens he had collected, he came to a startling conclusion: The reptiles, birds, fish, and insects existed nowhere but on those islands.

Darwin soon made another, equally important discovery. Although many of the islands were separated by no more than fifty miles, the species differed from island to island. The variations among the finches were the most striking. The birds of each island had

Lagenorhynchus sp.
short-beaked dolphin

Dusicyon griseus
Argentine grey fox

Felis iaguarondi
jaguarundi

Phaethornis eurunome
hermit hummingbird

Camarhynchus crassirostris
Darwin's tree finch

Polyborus plancus
carancho or crested caracara

Felis geoffroyi
Geoffroy's cat

clearly distinctive plumages and beaks.

Darwin did not immediately try to explain the phenomenon. Instead he turned the question over in his head: What could cause such variations? The answer would become the foundation of his theory of natural selection: Those creatures must have adapted over generations to the Galápagos's unique conditions and to the unique conditions of each individual isle.

Darwin's theory was simple and at the same time revolutionary. According to the Bible, animal species were created with fixed attributes and unchanging characteristics. If Darwin was correct, species were continually evolving.

51

THE MYSTERY OF THE CORALS

Darwin's discoveries came as he continually asked himself questions. The Galápagos supplied many of those questions, but his trip through the Andes had been equally significant. Darwin couldn't sleep for wondering about the origins of those gigantic ridges.

The Bible's explanation was that the Earth's mountains, rivers, and plains had been formed by the Great Flood. Darwin believed that the Andes's granite core had risen through a series of tremendous upheavals. How long had the process taken? Even FitzRoy put aside his traditional Christian beliefs to let Darwin convince him that those peaks and plateaus had taken longer than the Flood's forty days to form.

If continental America was rising, Darwin thought, the ocean floor must be sinking. He hoped to find evidence of this phenomenon in the coral atolls scattered across the Pacific. FitzRoy, meanwhile, would try to determine whether the coral formations rested on the craters of extinct volcanoes that, themselves,

rested on the ocean floor.

With these unanswered questions, Darwin and the *Beagle* arrived in Tahiti. There Darwin didn't limit himself to studying corals. He was fascinated by Tahiti's luxuriant vegetation: bananas; coconut, palm, and breadfruit trees; pineapples. He liked the Tahitian people as well. He was struck by their vividly colored shirts and *pareos*, a type of wraparound skirt. He admired the elegant women with camelias behind their ears. There were Tahitians alive who remembered Captain Cook's arrival in the islands and who told stories of the mutiny on the ship *Bounty*.

There was also a reception on the ship in honor of Queen Pomare. With little gallantry Darwin described her as "an awkward large woman without any beauty, gracefulness or dignity of manners."

Darwin was fascinated by the vastness and the complexity of the coral reef. It was more than one thousand miles long and hosted hundreds of plant and animal species.

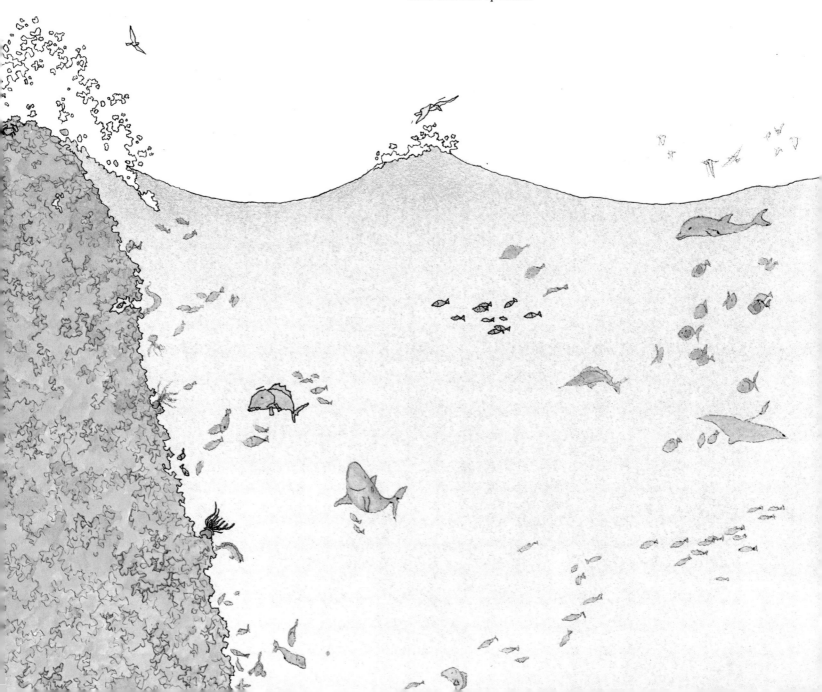

AUSTRALIA'S CONTRADICTIONS

The *Beagle* sailed onward across the Pacific. In December 1835 the ship reached New Zealand and a few weeks later, in January 1836, put into Sydney Cove at Port Jackson, Australia. The ship's company was stunned by Sydney's considerable size and wealth.

Darwin found the city unappealing. He quickly realized that Australian society was full of contradictions. The country had initially been populated by English convicts. Once freed, many of them prospered. There was a tense rivalry between the free colonists and the former prisoners. Australia's indigenous

In January 1836 the Beagle *put into Sydney Cove. Darwin and the crew ventured into the interior to explore the Australian continent.*

people, the aborigines, had been all but wiped out. Here was yet another proof that the arrival of European explorers and colonists was often fatal to local populations.

An expedition into the interior was more satisfying to Darwin. The flora did not interest him, but he was fascinated by the animals. He captured a kangaroo, the first marsupial he had ever seen. The birds, as well, astonished him.

At last it was time to return home. The *Beagle* put in at Mauritius, Capetown, Saint Helena, Ascension, and Brazil. Then, on October 2, 1836, the courageous crew sighted the English coast for the first time in five years.

Geochelone elaphantopus
Galápagos giant tortoise

Chlamyphorus retusus
armadillo

Ornithorhynchus anatinus
platypus

Amblyrhynchus cristatus
marine iguana

Trogon viridis
White-tailed trogon

Scorpaena sp.
scorpionfish

Dromaius baudinianus
Kangaroo Island emu

ENDANGERED ANIMALS

Of his stay in Australia, Darwin wrote, "Until a few years ago the country was full of wild animals, but now the emu has been driven back prohibitive distances, and the kangaroo has become rare. It may take some time, but the fate of these animals is sealed."

As often happened, his words proved prophetic. Although kangaroos have prospered, humans have hunted many other animals into near or total extinction. The process is not new. The ancient Romans, for example, seriously threatened the lion, elephant, and giraffe when they killed enormous numbers in their arenas for sport.

From Darwin's day until the present, the number of species threatened with extinction has grown. The con-

Conolophus subscristatus
Galápagos iguana

Saguinus oedipus
cotton-top tamarin

Scelorchilus albicollis
White-throated tapacolo

pouter pigeon

Bromelia bicolor

Lagorchestes sp.
hare wallaby

Neophoca cinerea
Australian sea lion (female)

temporary problem of air and water pollution is only the latest in a series of assaults on Earth's wildlife.

Darwin's reflections on Australia, however, were not confined to pessimistic predictions. He was fascinated by the island continent's marsupials. These mammals, which are found nowhere else on Earth, have a pouch on their stomach in which they carry their young for several months. Australia is believed to have broken off from Asia 60 million years ago. Darwin hypothesized that Australia's marsupials, in their isolation, retained their primitive pouch, whereas related mammals of Asia and elsewhere evolved beyond it.

With this hypothesis, Darwin advanced a step closer to his theory of evolution.

A MAN AND HIS STUDY

Charles Darwin was only twenty-seven years old when he reached London following his extraordinary voyage. All his life lay before him. Darwin was certain that he wanted to pass it studying and writing but uncertain of where to live. In London, as he humorously wrote, there was always fresh fish and fresh news. The countryside, however, would provide him with the quiet necessary for thought and meditation.

On May 29, 1839, four years after his return to England, he married a cousin, Emma Wedgwood. She was a model of domestic virtues and became a sort of governess to and protector of Darwin. She even nursed him through the migraines and mysterious illnesses from which he suffered all his life.

Charles and Emma settled in London, but London had the drawbacks of all large cities: noise, congestion, dirt. The newlyweds quickly retired to the countryside. They found a house, not luxurious but comfortable, in the village of Downe, in Kent, just two hours from London.

Major renovations were made to the house.

Particular care was taken with Darwin's study. It was a large room with two oversize windows that made it ideal for writing and for studying subjects under a microscope. There were fireplaces and comfortable armchairs. Most important, the room was removed from the noises and bustle of the rest of the house. In this placid spot Darwin ordered the thoughts that would soon disrupt contemporary society.

The first of his numerous books was the account of his voyage on the *Beagle*: *Diary of a Naturalist Around the World*. It was published in 1839 to great acclaim and subsequently appeared in numerous foreign editions. Darwin even received an enthusiastic note from no less a personage than Alexander von Humboldt. This praise from his greatest hero gave Darwin immense joy.

Downe was a pleasant spot. Darwin would remain there for the rest of his long life, seeing few friends, taking walks, but above all studying and writing. He had ten children, seven of whom survived him. He was described as the most affectionate and attentive of fathers.

Darwin's study in the house at Downe was undoubtedly the room most dear to him. He passed most of his days there, studying and writing.

Although he was a member of the Royal Society, the most prestigious British academy, Darwin rarely spent time there.

THE GREAT RECLUSE

Darwin very quickly clarified the ideas that led to his theory of evolution based on natural selection. The first notebooks containing specific references were those of 1837. Darwin confessed that he was already "obsessed by the fact that the varieties of life on our planet have departed from their ancestral forms."

The Bible, however, stated the opposite. According to Genesis, the world of Darwin's time was identical to the world that God had created in six days. Darwin was a member of the Anglican church. How could he publicly claim that the story of Adam and Eve was a fable? He prudently delayed publishing his opinions.

Instead, Darwin spent his life working in seclusion. He had few social contacts. Although he was a member of the Royal Society, he spent little time there, preferring to take long contemplative walks in the quiet of his property. In 1858, however, an event occurred that would change his life. Darwin received a letter from Alfred Russel Wallace accompanied by an essay entitled "On the Tendency of Varieties to Depart Indefinitely from the Original Type."

This was a blow indeed. Wallace, a traveler and naturalist, expressed ideas that paralleled Darwin's own thoughts. With characteristic generosity, Darwin forwarded the essay to the noted scientist Charles Lyell for formal presentation. He added ruefully, "So all my originality . . . will be smashed." But his years of work would not, as he feared, be wasted. Wallace's essay was presented to the Linnaean Society of London, and Darwin's work was published as a book.

On the Origin of Species by Means of Natural Selection appeared in 1859. All 1,250 copies sold out on the day it was published. The book's theories instantly became the subject of heated debate.

Darwin published many other studies, including *The Variation of Animals and Plants under Domestication, The Descent of Man and Selection in Relation to Sex,* and *The Expression of the Emotions in Man and Animals.* He also wrote an autobiography.

Darwin loved the quiet of Kent, where he walked for hours in solitude.

THE PROBLEM OF EVOLUTION

Since ancient times, people have theorized on the origins of life. Theories generally fall into one of two categories: those that support the idea of unchanging species and those that support the idea that species evolved. Greek philosophy was evolutionary in nature. Just prior to Darwin's time, such scientists as Buffon, Lamarck, and Darwin's own grandfather,

individuals of each species are born than can survive, and as consequently there is frequently recurring a struggle for existence, it follows that any being, if it vary however slightly in any manner profitable to itself . . . will have a better chance of surviving and thus be naturally selected. This preservation of favourable individual differences and the variations, and the destruction of those which are injurious, I have called Natural Selection, or the Survival of the Fittest."

According to Darwin's theory, humans and apes derived from a common ancestral family and evolved apart over millennia.

Australopithecus aferensis

Australopithecus robustus

Australopithecus boisei

Erasmus Darwin, advanced theories on evolutionary change.

Charles Darwin's concept of natural selection was considered so original, however, as to have created a separate theory: Darwinism. He stated the underlying principles thus: "As many more

Thomas Malthus had been an important influence on Darwin's thinking. According to Malthus, populations increased geometrically while food supplies increased in a simple arithmetic progression. Living beings were thus forced into a struggle for survival. This struggle, which ensured the success of the best adapted, was, according to Darwin, the mechanism through which species changed. Indeed, a species improved its chances of survival in direct proportion to the number of individual variations it included.

Darwin's most provocative ideas concerned human origins. Darwin was widely thought to believe that humans were descended through a series of adaptations from apes. Darwin never

was harsh. In the notorious Oxford meeting of 1860, Bishop Samuel Wilberforce exchanged insults with Darwin's supporter, T. H. Huxley. Wilberforce was not alone in criticizing Darwinism. Darwin himself, a man of absolute intellectual honesty, had doubts and second thoughts about his theories until the end of his life.

Although Charles Darwin received no state honors while he lived, his fame was enormous.

Homo habilis   Homo erectus

Homo sapiens

supported this thesis. Instead he believed that contemporary humans, Homo sapiens, and anthropoid apes had evolved over millennia from a common ancestral family.

It was enough, however, that Darwin contradicted the Bible. The reaction in some quarters

When he died, on April 19, 1882, he was buried at Westminster Abbey. Today he is recognized as the person who grasped the common origin of all living things and who placed humans within the natural world as one species among many.

PLANT HUNTERS

Linnaeus, whose legacy to modern science is a system of plant and animal classification, wrote: "The acts of heroism accomplished by scholars of botany are in no way inferior to those of great kings, heroes, and emperors. Unfortunately they have not been recognized."

If we consider the efforts of thousands of amateur naturalists to obtain rare plant specimens, Linnaeus's words do not seem an exaggeration. Ernest Wilson provides a good example. From 1899 on, Wilson traversed vast regions of China to obtain plants for European nurseries and collectors. One day, while searching a mountainous region for a certain species of lily, his expedition was caught in an avalanche. A boulder fractured Wilson's leg in two places.

Wilson realized that without care gangrene could set in. His only hope was to reach a doctor many days' travel away. He fashioned a temporary splint from the tripod of his camera and, with the help of porters, set out along the narrow mountain path while new avalanches rumbled around him.

A caravan composed of dozens of mules appeared, traveling in the opposite direction. There was not room on the path for all. Wilson realized he would have to turn back and lose time that could well prove fatal. The explorer made a desperate decision. He lay down on the path to let the mules pass over him. They stepped carefully, and he was not trampled. Wilson resumed his journey, reached the doctor, and saved his life.

Wilson's adventure demonstrates the enormous demand that existed in Europe for exotic plants. Hundreds of professionals sent by botanic gardens or by nurseries scoured Asia and the tropics looking for plants and seeds. In the European capitals and in New York, single plants and plant collections became so important that they were sold at auctions as precious objects. At first the focus was on such fragile plants as orchids, which needed costly hothouses to survive. As tastes changed, people began to create gardens with hardy exotic plants that could endure winters outdoors.

In this way, gardens became available to all.

Beginning in 1899, botanist Ernest Wilson spent many years in China. Living conditions were often difficult as he sought rare plants for European nurseries.

MONET'S GARDEN

The contemporary North American and European garden is vastly different from that of past periods. The number of plants that began arriving in the West in the nineteenth century from all parts of the world forever altered our landscape. Color triumphed in the

The painter Claude Monet declared, "What I need is flowers, always." His garden at Giverny is represented in more than five hundred of his paintings.

garden, and informality replaced the rigid geometrical layouts of the past.

One of Europe's most famous gardens belonged to the great French painter Claude Monet (1840-1926). Monet, a founder of the impressionist movement, painted in the open air of the French countryside. At Giverny, in the Epte River valley, he created a garden to which he devoted himself for half of his long life. There he freely mixed plants and colors. His pond is particularly well known for containing the water lilies that appear repeatedly in his paintings. Monet's garden had a bridge in the Oriental style. It was painted green rather than the traditional red because the artist considered green more suitable to the setting. Today Giverny is open to the public. It is as lovely now as it was in Monet's time.

STUDYING THE OCEANS

The study of the oceans, their ecosystems, flora, and fauna, has not kept pace with land-based studies. To be sure, seafaring peoples always enjoyed a special relationship with the ocean. The Polynesians sailed extensive routes on the Pacific without navigational instruments. Europeans, from the Vikings to Columbus, navigated with only the most rudimentary equipment. These seafarers relied on generations of experience with the sea, its winds, currents, and changes of color. They recognized the significance of birds' flight patterns and the movement of clouds. Familiarity with the ocean did nothing to lessen their awe of it.

Early sailors' aims were practical rather than scientific. Even the voyage of the *Beagle* was undertaken primarily to improve commercial routes. Early ocean exploration consisted mainly of charting geography.

Gradually, however, explorers began to raise questions regarding the nature of the oceans: water temperature and density; light penetration; chemical composition; the composition of the ocean floor; and so forth.

The first marine expedition with scientific interests was by the British ship *Challenger*, which left port on December 21, 1872. The *Challenger* was a three-masted ship with an auxiliary motor typical of the period, but it also had a number of improvements. It contained an up-to-date chemical laboratory, a biology lab, and equipment to sound the ocean floor and dredge it. It eventually covered almost seventy thousand nautical miles, generated much public interest, and gave birth to the science of oceanography.

After the *Challenger*, oceanography became an important field of scientific research. The first oceanographic institutes were founded to sponsor expeditions and other research. The result is that today more than a thousand floating laboratories ply the waves. Their data have been used to find petroleum, to lay undersea cables, and to chart the movements of fish. Unfortunately it also shows that the world's waters are becoming increasingly polluted.

From 1872 to 1876 the Challenger, sponsored by the British Royal Society, completed the first expedition to study the physics, chemistry, biology, and geography of the oceans.

DEEPER INTO THE SEA

One of civilization's oldest questions has been, What lies at the bottom of the ocean? Easier questions such as, What is the composition of seawater? and What lies beyond this ocean? were more readily answered. Advanced technology was required to allow humans to descend to the oceans' depths. Only in recent decades has that technology become available.

Prior centuries produced numerous designs for submarine vessels, including one by Leonardo da Vinci. None was built until a first timid attempt at undersea exploration was made in 1690 by the noted astronomer Edmund Halley. Halley designed a primitive diving bell, actually a bottomless barrel, into which air was pumped.

Was there life in the depths?

The answer came in 1858 when the first subterranean cable was laid on the ocean floor. The cable was soon covered with plants

Auguste Piccard's bathyscaphe, Trieste.

and organisms, proof that life existed even at the greatest depths.

In the twentieth century a series of undersea vessels, bathyscaphes, were built to withstand the enormous pressures of the lower depths. Auguste Piccard's bathyscaphe, *Trieste*, descended the farthest. Piccard and his son, Jacques, built the vessel and in 1953 piloted it to 10,332 feet below sea level.

The French naval officer Jacques Yves Cousteau gave undersea exploration a huge boost when he founded a research group in 1944. Cousteau invented a special diving suit and an underwater movie camera. One of his films, *The Silent World*, received a prize at the Cannes Film Festival. Thanks to Cousteau millions of people have witnessed life unfolding in the ocean's depths.

Some vessels used to explore and study the undersea world since the 1950s.

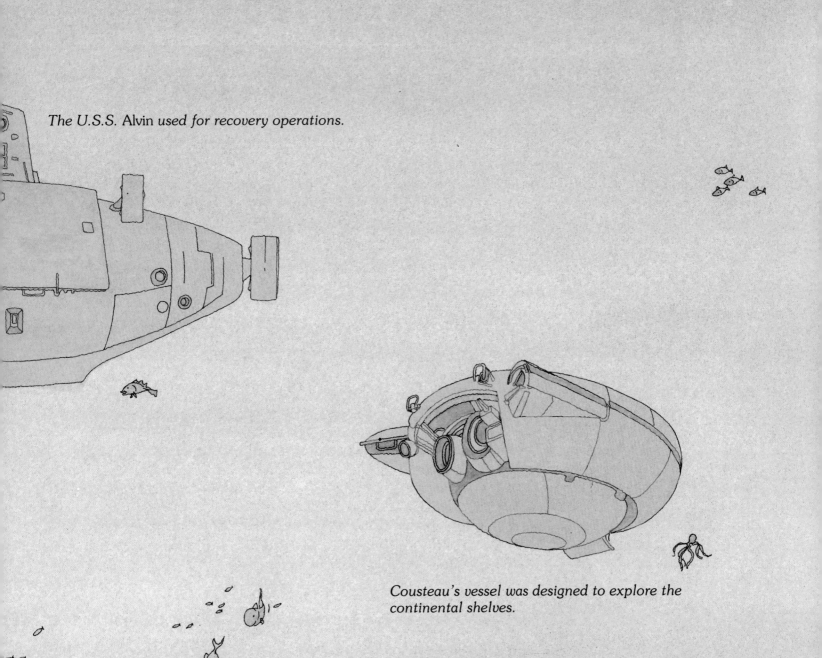

The U.S.S. Alvin *used for recovery operations.*

Cousteau's vessel was designed to explore the continental shelves.

THE SOUTH POLE

For centuries the southern oceans were believed to hide a vast and mysterious continent. It took the voyages of Captain Cook in the second half of the eighteenth century to discredit the idea that islands such as New Guinea and New Zealand were part of this unknown continent.

Antarctica's existence was firmly established only in 1840, by James Ross's expedition aboard the ships *Erebus* and *Terror*. Ross's diary is full of awestruck accounts unique to discoverers of the unknown.

Ross described Antarctic icebergs, in contrast to those of the Arctic, as platelike and gigantic. They were 150 to 200 feet high, with perimeters approaching two miles. The expedition encountered baleen and sperm whales that "seemed almost tame so unafraid were they as our ships slipped among them." Seals lazed on the ice. So did penguins, birds found only in the Southern Hemisphere.

Ross named a volcano, Erebus, for one of his ships. He discovered the giant ice barrier that bears his name, the Ross Shelf Ice. At two hundred feet in height and four hundred miles in length, the shelf made, and makes, farther progress by ship impossible. Expeditions that seek to reach the South Pole must proceed from the Ross Shelf Ice onto the vast ice pack by dogsled.

The challenge to reach the South Pole turned into a race between Roald Amundsen, who arrived in December 1911, and Robert Scott, who reached it in January 1912.

Antarctica has an area of 5.5 million square miles. The initial race to reach the Pole was an adventure of high drama. British explorer Robert Scott and Norwegian Roald Amundsen led rival expeditions. Scott set out in the summer of 1910 with an expedition that included several scientists. He did not bring dogs to pull his sleds because he had seen dogs die on a previous expedition. In a decision that would prove fateful, he brought horses as pack animals instead.

On January 18, 1912, after having overcome dangers, hardships, and the death of the horses, Scott and his team reached the bottom of the world. A terrible disappointment awaited them. They found a sled with a Norwegian flag flying. Amundsen's party, following a different route, had arrived at the Pole with their three sleds and fifty-two dogs a month earlier, on December 14, 1911. The worst was still to come for Scott. He and his companions were exhausted from pulling their heavy loads. Their hands and feet were half frozen. The company took refuge in a small tent on the ice pack and died there.

The recently opened Amundsen-Scott Station memorializes the notable contributions of both historic expeditions with an up-to-date research center. Antarctica is no longer a mystery. During International Geophysical Year, in 1958, the world's governments agreed that Antarctica would be preserved for scientific research rather than fought over and exploited for its resources.

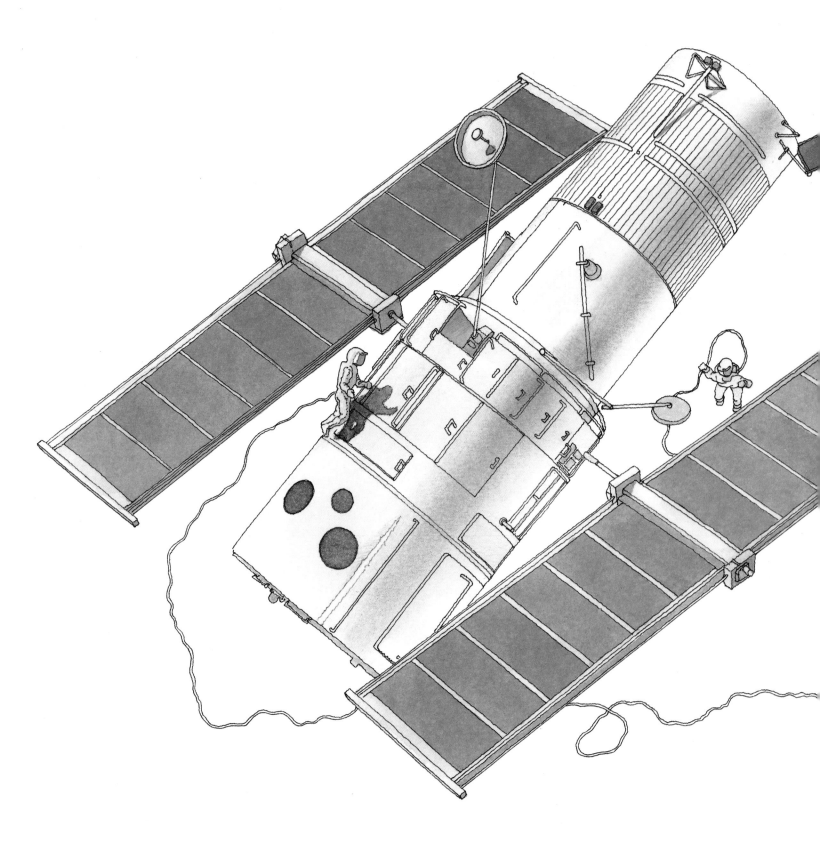

The space telescope Hubble, mounted on the space shuttle. Despite initial problems with its lenses, the Hubble is considered one of the technological marvels of the twentieth century. It will let us glimpse the very ends of the universe, 14 million light years away.

THE NATURE OF THE STARS

Now that we have solved many of the mysteries of our planet, we have turned our attention increasingly in the last few decades to space. On July 21, 1969, an American astronaut, Neil Armstrong, became the first human being to set foot on the moon. Prior to that, in 1959, a Soviet satellite had orbited Earth and

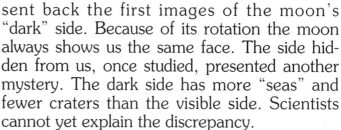

sent back the first images of the moon's "dark" side. Because of its rotation the moon always shows us the same face. The side hidden from us, once studied, presented another mystery. The dark side has more "seas" and fewer craters than the visible side. Scientists cannot yet explain the discrepancy.

Today our heavens swarm with space stations, probes, and satellites. Spaceships have made voyages to other planets of our solar system and sent back data that reveal much about Earth's distant neighbors. We know that Jupiter is a gaseous giant, that Uranus has fifteen moons, that Saturn's famous rings are composed of thousands of ice fragments, that Mars is the most similar in dimensions to Earth, and that Neptune is buffeted by the fastest winds of the entire system. Venus, the hottest planet, suffers from the "greenhouse" effect that threatens Earth; its surface is battered by acid rains.

The space shuttle is the latest advance in space exploration. It has the major advantage of being reusable. All space vehicles are prohibitively expensive, but the shuttle is more cost-effective than most. Because it returns to Earth after each voyage, its major expense is its fuel.

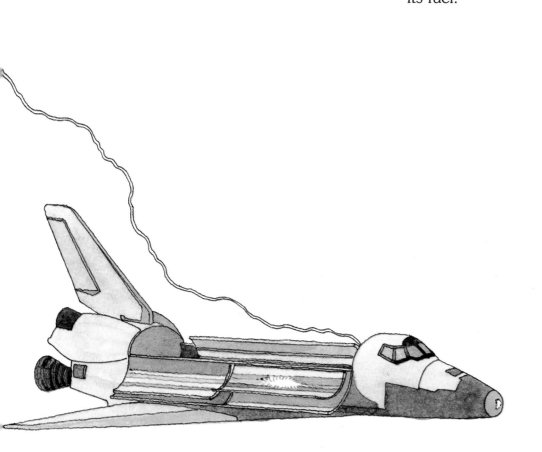

Index